ABOUT THE BANK STREET READY-TO-READ SERIES

More than seventy-five years of educational research, innovative teaching, and quality publishing have earned The Bank Street College of Education its reputation as America's most trusted name in early childhood education.

Because no two children are exactly alike in their development, the Bank Street Ready-to-Read series is written on three levels to accommodate the individual stages of reading readiness of children ages three through eight.

○ *Level 1:* GETTING READY TO READ (Pre-K–Grade 1)

Level 1 books are perfect for reading aloud with children who are getting ready to read or just starting to read words or phrases. These books feature large type, repetition, and simple sentences.

● *Level 2:* READING TOGETHER (Grades 1–3)

These books have slightly smaller type and longer sentences. They are ideal for children beginning to read by themselves who may need help.

○ *Level 3:* I CAN READ IT MYSELF (Grades 2–3)

These stories are just right for children who can read independently. They offer more complex and challenging stories and sentences.

All three levels of the Bank Street Ready-to-Read books make it easy to select the books most appropriate for your child's development and enable him or her to grow with the series step by step. The levels purposely overlap to reinforce skills and further encourage reading.

We feel that making reading fun is the single most important thing anyone can do to help children become good readers. We hope you will become part of Bank Street's long tradition of learning through sharing.

The Bank Street College of Education

To Ellen,
for sharing
— J.K.

For Scott
— L.R.

For a free color catalog describing Gareth Stevens' list of high-quality books and multimedia programs, call 1-800-542-2595 (USA) or 1-800-461-9120 (Canada). Gareth Stevens Publishing's Fax: (414) 225-0377.

Library of Congress Cataloging-in-Publication Data

Kindley, Jeffrey.
    Scamper's year / by Jeff Kindley; illustrated by Laura Rader.
      p. cm. -- (Bank Street ready-to-read)
    Summary: Scamper the squirrel enjoys each season, from spring's bright flowers to summer picnics, colorful autumn leaves, and winter's blanket of snow.
    ISBN 0-8368-1777-X (lib. bdg.)
    1. Squirrels--Juvenile fiction. [1. Squirrels--Fiction. 2. Seasons--Fiction.]
    I. Rader, Laura, ill. II. Title. III. Series.
    PZ10.3.K556Sc 1999
    [E]--dc21   98-38482

This edition first published in 1999 by
Gareth Stevens Publishing
1555 North RiverCenter Drive, Suite 201
Milwaukee, Wisconsin 53212 USA

© 1997 by Byron Preiss Visual Publications, Inc. Text © 1997 by Bank Street College of Education. Illustrations © 1997 by Laura Rader and Byron Preiss Visual Publications, Inc.

Published by arrangement with Bantam Doubleday Dell Books For Young Readers, a division of Bantam Doubleday Dell Publishing Group, Inc., New York, New York. All rights reserved.

Bank Street Ready To Read ™ is a registered U.S. trademark of the Bank Street Group and Bantam Doubleday Dell Books For Young Readers, a division of Bantam Doubleday Dell Publishing Group, Inc.

Printed in Mexico

1 2 3 4 5 6 7 8 9 03 02 01 00 99

Bank Street Ready-to-Read™

Scamper's Year

by Jeff Kindley
Illustrated by Laura Rader

A Byron Preiss Book

Gareth Stevens Publishing
MILWAUKEE

Early in spring,
Scamper the baby squirrel
peeks out of his nest
for the very first time.

He looks down from his treetop
through branches
covered with tiny green leaves.

Way down below
kids play hide-and-seek
and swing on the swings.

They shout and chase each other
past bright yellow daffodils.
"Can't catch *me*!" they laugh,
and they race away.

Soon Scamper is big enough
to play games.
He chases the other squirrels
up and down the tree trunks.

"Hey, look!" yells one of the kids.
"The squirrels can play tree tag!"
But none of the squirrels
can catch Scamper.

Scamper the acrobat
loves showing off.
He bounces from branch to branch
and swings from tree to tree.

Sometimes he just likes
to hang upside down,
enjoying the sweet spring breeze.

What could be better than spring?

Whoosh!
The sprinklers spout
cool, clear water that
makes rainbows in the air.

It's summer!
Kids dash through the sprinkler,
screaming and laughing.

Scamper keeps cool in the sun
by shading himself
under his big, bushy tail.

Mmm, what's this?
Scamper follows delicious smells
to a picnic on the grass.

He tiptoes closer
to watch the people eat.
They toss him sunflower seeds
and bites of their sandwiches.

He grabs the food in his paws
and quickly nibbles it up.
Scamper loves summer picnics!

What could be better than summer?

Whist!
A shivery wind whistles by.
The leaves on the trees turn
yellow and red and orange.
It's fall.

Crunchy leaves drift down
onto the grass.
The kids push them into piles
and take turns jumping in them.

The kids run and shout
in the crisp fall air.
To Scamper, their football
looks like a great big
delicious nut.

Mmm!
Nuts and acorns everywhere!
The squirrels dart around
to pick up all they can.

They crack some open
with their sharp teeth
and bury the rest for winter.

Eating all those nuts
makes Scamper chubby.

What could be better than fall?

Brrrr!
Scamper sleeps in his nest,
using his tail as a blanket.
He's safe and warm and snug.
It's winter.

The whole park looks like
it's sleeping too.
A big white blanket of snow
covers everything.

Scamper wakes up hungry.
It's time to dig up all those nuts
he buried last fall.

Girls and boys are sledding
and making angels in the snow.
They all wear heavy winter coats,
just like Scamper.

And they bring a surprise
for their friends the squirrels:
a feeder full of nuts and seeds
and peanut butter.

Scamper likes
this winter picnic best of all!

What could be better than winter?

Drip, drip.
The snow and icicles melt.
Tiny green leaves uncurl again
on Scamper's tree.
It's spring.

A new baby squirrel
opens her eyes
in the nest of leaves.
Scamper has a sister!

Spring, summer, fall, and winter.
What will be her favorite season?

What's yours?